THE RABBIT'S
WHISKERS
AND OTHER STORIES

The Rabbit's Whiskers

and Other Stories

by
ENID BLYTON

Illustrated by
Suzy-Jane Tanner

AWARD PUBLICATIONS

For further information on Enid Blyton please contact www.blyton.com

ISBN 0-86163-182-X

Text copyright 1945 The Enid Blyton Company
Illustrations copyright © 1987 Award Publications Limited

Enid Blyton's signature is a trademark of The Enid Blyton Company

First published 1945 as *The Conjuring Wizard and Other Stories*
by Macmillan and Co. Limited

This edition entitled *The Rabbit's Whiskers and Other Stories*
published by permission of The Enid Blyton Company

First published 1987
13th impression 2001

Published by Award Publications Limited,
27 Longford Street, London NW1 3DZ

Printed in Singapore

CONTENTS

1

The Conjuring Wizard

Jimmy was dreadfully disappointed. He had been asked to a party that day, and now here he was in bed with a cold! It really was too bad.

Mummy was very sorry for him. 'Cheer up, darling,' she said. 'There will be lots more parties.'

'Yes, but this one is going to have a conjurer,' said Jimmy. 'Just think of that, Mummy! Oh, I do wish I was going to see him.'

7

Mummy looked so sad to think that he was in bed, that Jimmy made up his mind to be cheerful about the party, and to pretend he didn't really mind. So he lay in bed smiling, and tried not to mind when he heard the children arriving at the party next door.

Mummy brought him his tea, and when he had finished it he lay back in bed, half asleep. Suddenly he heard a knock at the door, and he called out: 'Come in!' thinking that perhaps it was Jane, the maid.

But it wasn't. It was a strange-looking man in a high, pointed hat. He wore a cloak, and on it were stars and half-moons.

'Good evening,' he said to the surprised little boy. I heard you were not very well, so I came along to see you. Do you feel very dull?'

'It is a bit dull lying in bed with a cold when you know there's a party next door with a conjurer,' said Jimmy.

'A conjurer!' said the man. 'Do you like conjurers?'

8

'I should just think I do!' said Jimmy. 'Why, at a party I went to last year there was a conjurer who made some goldfish come out of a silk handkerchief and swim in a glass of water. And there was nothing in that handkerchief, because it was mine that I had had clean for the party!'

'Pooh, that's nothing!' said the strange-looking man. I can make goldfish come out of the pocket of your pyjamas and swim in your tea-cup!'

9

'You couldn't !' said Jimmy.

'Well, look here, then!' said the man, and he suddenly put his hand into Jimmy's pocket, took out three wriggly goldfish and popped them into the little boy's tea-cup, which suddenly became full of water. The fish swam about gaily, then leapt up into the air and vanished.

'Ooh!' said Jimmy, astonished. 'How did you do that?'

'Aha!' said the man. 'I can do much cleverer things than that!'

'Then you must be a wizard,' said Jimmy.

'Perhaps I am,' said the man with a laugh. 'Just give me your handkerchief, will you?' Jimmy gave it to him. The wizard folded it neatly into four and laid it on the bed. 'There's nothing in it, is there?' he said to Jimmy. 'Just feel and see.'

Jimmy felt. No, the handkerchief was quite soft and flat. The wizard picked it up and shook it out with a laugh. Out ran a white rabbit – and another – and another – and another!

'Goodness!' gasped Jimmy, amazed. 'However did they get there? Ooh, look at them running all over the room!'

The rabbits ran here and there, and suddenly popped up the chimney.

'They have gone,' said the conjurer. 'Now I'll do another trick. Open your mouth, Jimmy.'

Jimmy opened it, and to his great surprise the wizard began to pull coloured paper out of it. More and more he pulled, till the bed was full of it. Jimmy shut his mouth at last, and looked at the paper in astonishment.

'Well!' he said, 'I can't think how my mouth held all that, really I can't. Do another trick, Mr. Conjurer.'

'I'll make the poker and shovel do a dance together,' said the conjurer. He waved his hands, and suddenly the poker and the shovel each grew two spindly legs and two thin arms. Then they began to dance. How funny it was to see them! They bowed and kicked, jumped and sprang, and Jimmy laughed till the tears came into his eyes.

'Now do another trick,' he said.

Then the wizard did a strange thing. He picked up the coal-scuttle and emptied all the coal on the bed!

'Oh, you mustn't do that,' said Jimmy. 'Mummy will be cross!'

'It's all right!' said the conjurer. 'Did you think it was coal? Well, it's not!'

And to Jimmy's great astonishment he saw that the lumps of coal had all turned into toys! There was a fine clockwork engine, a ship with a sail, a picture book, a box of soldiers and an aeroplane.

'Good gracious!' cried Jimmy, 'what fun!'

The wizard waved his hands once more. The engine leapt off the bed and ran round the floor. The ship jumped into Jimmy's wash-basin and sailed there. The soldiers sprang out of their box and marched up and down the bed in a line. The aeroplane flew round and round in the air, and the book began to read the stories aloud!

The Conjuring Wizard

'You are a marvellous man!' cried Jimmy. 'Do tell me who you are and where you come from.'

'Very well,' said the conjurer, and he sat down in the chair by Jimmy's bed. 'My name is ...'

But just at that very minute there came another knock at Jimmy's door. The conjurer straightaway jumped through the window and vanished. The toys flew into the coal-scuttle and became coal, and the coloured paper shrivelled up and disappeared in the twinkling of an eye.

The door opened and the doctor came in with Mummy.

'Hallo, hallo,' he said. 'And how are we feeling now?'

'He's looking better,' said Mummy. 'Why, Jimmy, you look quite excited. Anyone would think you had been seeing the conjurer after all!'

'And so I have!' said Jimmy. Then he told the Doctor and Mummy all about the marvellous wizard. But they didn't believe him at all. And then Jimmy suddenly saw one of the rabbits! It came popping down the chimney and jumped up on the bed.

'You must believe me now, Mummy!' he said, 'for look, here's one of the rabbits!'

Jimmy still has that rabbit. Isn't he lucky?

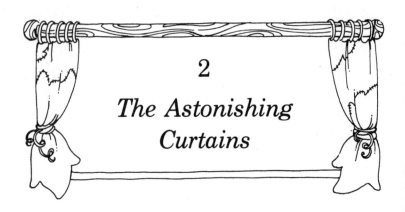

2

The Astonishing Curtains

Mary had a lovely doll's house. When Grandma gave it to her for her birthday it was quite new and empty. Grandpa gave her one pound to buy furniture for it, and Auntie Susan gave her fifty pence to buy curtains.

Mary went to the toy shop and spent the pound. She bought a little wooden table for the kitchen and two chairs to match. She bought a kitchen stove and dresser and some tiny saucepans and a kettle.

She bought little beds for the bedrooms, and wardrobes and chairs. She even bought a washstand for the biggest bedroom of all. The dining-room had a round table, four chairs and a sideboard, and the drawing room had a fine carpet, a sofa, three pretty chairs and a tiny table.

Well, you wouldn't think she could get all those for a pound, would you? But she did, because the things only cost three or four pence each, and, as I daresay you know, there are one hundred pence in one pound, which is really rather a lot to spend all at once!

'Don't buy the stuff for the curtains today,' said Nurse. 'You'll have plenty to do arranging all the things you've bought. We will buy the curtains another time, and then I will help you to make them, and hang them up. You can keep Auntie Susan's fifty pence until you want to buy the curtains.'

Mary arranged all her new furniture in the doll's house, and it did look nice. It took her four days to get it all in and

The Astonishing Curtains

to lay the carpets and bits of oil cloth. Then she took out her fifty pence piece, and decided to buy the stuff for the curtains.

She spun it on the nursery floor – but, oh dear me, when it stopped spinning, it rolled away and disappeared down a hole in one of the boards by the wall. Mary called Nurse, but they couldn't get it.

'No, it's gone,' said Nurse. 'It's a mousehole, I expect, and unless we have some boards taken up, you won't get your money back again. I'm sure your Daddy won't have the boards up, so you must make up your mind that it's gone for good.'

Tears came to Mary's eyes.

'What about the curtains for the doll's house?' she said. 'I've finished it all except for those – and Grandma and Auntie Susan are coming next week to see my house all finished.'

'Well, you shouldn't have been so careless as to lose your fifty pence,' said Nurse. 'I told you to put it safely in your money-box.'

She went out of the room and Mary sat down on the floor and cried. It really was too disappointing for anything. She did so badly want pretty red curtains to hang at the windows of the doll's house.

That night, when the nursery was quiet, and Mary had gone to bed, the toys in the cupboard came trooping out. And dear me, they were so cross with the little clockwork mouse!

'It's all your fault that Mary lost her fifty pence,' said the panda, angrily.

'What do you mean?' asked the clockwork mouse in surprise.

'Well, your friend, the little brown mouse from the garden, made that hole to come into the nursery and visit you,' said the panda, pointing to the hole. 'And it was down his hole that Mary's money went. If you hadn't wanted that mouse to come and see you, he wouldn't have made that hole, and Mary wouldn't have lost her fifty pence!'

The clockwork mouse was dreadfully upset. He began to cry, and the toys tried to stop him, because they were afraid his tears might rust his spring.

'I w-w-wish I c-c-could get M-M-Mary some nice n-n-new curtains!' he sobbed. 'I'm so s-s-sorry about it.'

'If only we could get some stuff, I could make them on that little toy sewing-machine Mary had for Christmas,' said the biggest doll. 'It wouldn't take me long, because I know quite well how to use it.'

'Well, where can we get some stuff?' asked the clockwork mouse, eagerly. 'I know Mary wanted red curtains – where can we get something that is red?'

'I know!' cried the teddy bear. 'What about the red creeper leaves that grow over the garden shed? If we got some of those, we could make lovely curtains from them for Mary.'

'But how can we get them?' asked the clockwork mouse.

'We'll ask your friend, the little brown garden mouse, to get them for us,' said the doll. So when the mouse popped up through the hole, they told him all about Mary and the lost fifty pence, and asked him to get the red leaves. First of all he tried to get the money out of the hole, but he couldn't. When he found it was no use, he ran off to get the red creeper

24

leaves. He came back with two beautiful ones in his mouth and then ran off for more.

The sewing-machine began to hum as the doll made the curtains. As soon as a pair were made the teddy bear and the panda took them to a window and put them up. You can't think how lovely they looked!

Just as the cock crowed at dawn, the last pair were finished and the toys went happily back to the toy cupboard.

And in the morning, when Mary came running into the nursery, oh, what a surprise she had! She stood and stared at the doll's house with its gay red curtains as if she really couldn't believe her eyes! And when she saw that they were made of red creeper leaves, she looked round at her smiling toys in wonder.

'You must have made them for me!' she said. 'You darlings!' She hugged them all tightly, and they were as pleased as could be.

'Now the house is all ready for grandma to see!' Mary cried. 'And the curtains are the prettiest part of all!'

3

Tick-a-Tock,
the Greedy Rabbit

There was once a rabbit called Tick-a-Tock, who found three gold pieces lying in the sunshine. They shone and glittered, and Tick-a-Tock thought they were very beautiful.

'Now I am rich,' he said, and he felt very proud. He took the gold pieces to his burrow, and hid them there. Sometimes he took them out and counted them – one, two, three – three, two, one! And sometimes he counted them over and over again, until he came to the number one hundred and pretended he was very rich indeed.

'I won't spend them,' he said. 'If I do, I shan't be rich any longer. I'll just keep them here to look at.'

Soon he began to wish that he had more than three. How exciting it would be if he had twelve to count! My! Wouldn't he be a rich rabbit!

'But how could I get some more?' he wondered. He thought and thought, and for a long time he couldn't think of any plan at all.

He was a silly rabbit, for he didn't need any money, not even a penny. He didn't have to pay for the grass he ate, nor for the tree-bark he sharpened his teeth on, nor for the cosy burrow he lived in. He didn't have to pay for the sunshine that warmed him nor for the wind that cooled him. He just wanted the money to make him feel rich!

At last he thought of a good plan.

'I will do odd jobs for everyone,' he said. 'Then I will charge people a gold piece, and I shall soon have as many as I want.'

So he put up a notice outside his

burrow which said:

ODD JOBS DONE.
APPLY INSIDE TODAY.

Then he waited for his customers to come.

Now many fairies lived round about Tick-a-Tock's home, and when they saw the rabbit's notice they were pleased. Tick-a-Tock hadn't a very good name for kindness, and the fairies all thought that he was turning over a new leaf, and was ready to do good turns to anyone. So the news soon went round that the rabbit would do all kinds of jobs – but nobody guessed that he meant to charge

them gold pieces.

First of all Sammy Squirrel called on him, and begged him to act as postman for the day.

'I'm having a party,' he said, 'and there are so many invitations that I haven't time to take them all round myself, or I shall never get the jellies made.'

Tick-a-Tock jumped up at once, and took all the letters. He put them into his wallet, and started off. It didn't take him very long to deliver them, for a rabbit gets along very fast. The last invitation of all was one for himself, so he didn't have to deliver that. Then he went to Sammy Squirrel's.

'I've done your job,' he said. 'Now will you pay me please?'

'Pay you!' said Sammy, looking most surprised. 'Whoever heard of paying for a kindly deed, I should like to know! We're not human beings, you know – we can afford to do things just out of kindness, which is much nicer! You must be mad, Tick-a-Tock!'

'No, I'm not,' said the rabbit. 'That will be one gold piece, please, Sammy. Come on, pay me quickly.'

'I haven't got even a silver piece,' said Sammy, crossly, 'and I shouldn't give it to you, if I had. I thought you were turning over a new leaf, and were going to do good turns to us all for a change. You've been a mean little rabbit for a long time!'

That made Tick-a-Tock furious, and he stamped off, tearing up his invitation as he went. He vowed he would make Sammy pay up some time or other.

Next day Fuff-Fuff the fairy went to ask him if he would carry a new dandelion clock from the hedge to her house, as her old clock was no use. She was such a tiny fairy that the weight was too much for her.

Well, that was nothing to Tick-a-Tock! He picked a fine dandelion clock, and in two minutes had taken it to where Fuff-Fuff lived in a red toadstool, and had stood it in her little hall.

'Oh, you kind rabbit!' she said, and

kissed him on the nose.

'That little job will be one gold piece,' said Tick-a-Tock. Fuff-Fuff gave a scream, and then laughed.

'You must be having a joke!' she said. 'We don't expect to be paid for kind deeds in Fairyland.'

'Nonsense,' said Tick-aTock. 'One gold piece, please.'

Well, of course, Fuff-Fuff didn't give it to him. She simply shut her door in disgust, and wouldn't open it even when he banged twelve times on the knocker.

Tick-a-Tock, the Greedy Rabbit

The next morning Tippity the elf came to Tick-a-Tock and begged him to carry him to his cousin Pippo, who was very ill.

'I've flown all through the night,' said poor Tippity, 'and I feel too tired to go any further. Then I saw your notice, so I came here to see if you could help me.'

In a trice Tick-a-Tock had galloped off to Pippo's with Tippity on his back. It only took ten minutes to take him there, and Tippity was very grateful.

'I'll never forget what you've done,' he said.

'Well, you must pay me a gold piece, please,' said Tick-a-Tock.

'Good gracious!' said Tippity, in dismay. 'Why, I thought you did these things for kindness.'

'No, certainly not,' said Tick-a-Tock.

He didn't get his gold piece from Tippity though, for the elf meant to spend all his money on his ill cousin, and he wouldn't give the greedy rabbit even a penny. He ran into Pippo's house and banged the door.

Then Tick-a-Tock began to make himself a dreadful nuisance. He went to Sammy Squirrel's every single day and shouted for his money. He went to Fuff-Fuff's too, and Tippity's, and made such a fuss and bother about his wretched gold pieces that at last the worried little things managed to get enough money together and give him a gold piece each. Tick-a-Tock was delighted, for now he had six gold pieces to count.

But the news soon went round that he charged for his kind deeds, and no one came to his burrow any more. Then one day a dreadful thing happened to Tick-a-Tock.

He was running along through the wood when the wind was very high, and suddenly a tree came crashing down to the ground! Poor Tick-a-Tock was caught underneath one of the branches, and his leg was broken. He shouted for help, and who should come by but Sammy Squirrel!

'Oh dear, oh dear, he won't help me,' thought Tick-a-Tock. But he was quite mistaken. Sammy came running up, and in two twinks he had lifted the branch and set Tick-a-Tock free.

'Half a minute,' he said. 'I'll get someone to help me carry you home.'

He ran off, and brought back Tippity the Elf! Tick-a-Tock felt certain that Tippity wouldn't dream of helping him – but he did! He was dreadfully sorry about poor Tick-a-Tock's leg, and he and Sammy gently carried him home.

'You must have a nurse,' said Sammy, and he went to fetch one. Who should he bring back but Fuff-Fuff, the fairy! Tick-a-Tock felt certain she wouldn't stay with him – but she did, and a very good little nurse she made! She brought his meals to him, and looked after him well until his leg had mended and he could go about once more.

'How much do you charge?' he asked Fuff-Fuff, when she said good-bye to him. 'Oh dear me, nothing at all,' she said. 'It's fine to do a kind deed, and I couldn't think of charging you anything, Tick-a-Tock!'

Sammy and Tippity said just the same thing, and Tick-a-Tock suddenly began to feel very ashamed of himself.

'They might easily have charged me two gold pieces each!' he thought. 'I couldn't have said no, for they might have left me under that tree. Dear, dear, how very kind of them!'

The more he thought about things, the more ashamed he felt, and that night he got up and went to his store of gold pieces. He took three envelopes and put two pieces of gold into each. Then he ran to Sammy's and dropped one envelope into the letter-box. He did the same at Tippity's and Fuff-Fuff's, and then he went back home feeling very happy.

He didn't take down the notice outside his burrow. It is still there, and heaps of people go to him every day for help. For, you see, he doesn't charge anything at all now. He likes to do things for kindness, so no wonder he is the best loved rabbit in the whole of Fairyland. The Queen heard of his good deeds and knighted him; so if ever you want his help, be sure to address your letters to Sir Tick-a-Tock Rabbit, or they might not reach him!

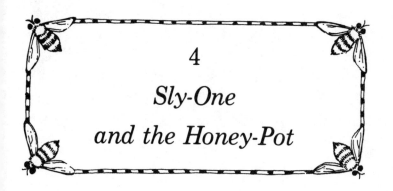

4

Sly-One
and the Honey-Pot

Fairy Sweet-Tooth kept fifteen hives of bees, for she was very fond of honey. When she took the honey from the comb, she put it in great big pots, and stood them in rows in a barn at the back of her house.

Next door to her lived Sly-One, the brownie. He was always trying to get honey from Sweet-Tooth for nothing, and she wouldn't give him any. She was very generous to her other neighbours, but then they were very kind to her.

The Saucepan-Man would always send her a new saucepan on her birthday, and the Ribbon-Woman nearly always gave her a lovely piece of green ribbon to match her best dress. And Sweet-Tooth was pleased to send them pots of honey in return.

But Sly-One never had a taste, and this made him very angry. He ought not to have expected any honey really, for he never did a good turn to Sweet-Tooth, and wouldn't even throw back her ball when it came into his garden.

Now one year the honey was very good indeed. It was so good that the honey barn at the back of the fairy's house was quite full of pots. In fact, even when Sweet-Tooth had given the Saucepan-Man two pots, and the Ribbon-Woman two, and sent three more to other people near, there was still not room for one of the pots in the barn. It stood outside, alone.

Sly-One saw it, and made up his mind that it was for him. So when he saw Sweet-Tooth that evening, he smiled his sweetest smile at her, and said:

'I see you have saved me a nice pot of honey, Sweet-Tooth. It is very kind of you.'

'It would be very kind of me if I had,' said Sweet-Tooth, 'but I haven't, Sly-One, and you know it. I don't like you or your ways, and I certainly don't mean to waste my honey on a deceitful little brownie like you!'

Well, that made Sly-One so angry that he was determined to get that extra pot if he possibly could – yes, and make some money out of it too!

So he went to the green elves that lived in the oak tree at the other end of the wood, and told them that if they liked he would sell them a pot of honey very cheaply. But they mustn't tell anyone, for it was a secret.

Sly-One knew that Sweet-Tooth went out on her pet snail at eleven o'clock every morning, and he thought that would be a good time to take the honey. But he didn't want anyone to think he had anything to do with it, so he laid his plans carefully.

'Come at eleven o'clock tomorrow,' he told the green elves. 'Go to the big barn you will see standing behind the house called 'Fairy Gables,' and outside the door you will see a large pot of honey left out for you. You can pay me when I call for the money.'

He hurried off, chuckling to himself. 'I'll be out when the elves call for the honey and take it away!' he said. 'They'll see the pot that can't be got into the shed because there's no room for it, and they'll think it's been left outside for them. So they'll take it and I'll get the money for it! I'll be sure to show myself at plenty of shops whilst the elves are taking the honey, and then no one will suspect me of having anything to do with it!'

So at eleven o'clock the next morning, when Sweet-Tooth started out on her pet snail with her little servant behind her, Sly-One went out too. He whistled loudly so that Sweet-Tooth should hear him, and he called in at lots of shops so that everyone saw him that morning. When he got home, Sweet-Tooth was crying.

'What's the matter?' he asked.

'Someone's stolen that lovely big pot of honey that stood outside my barn. Did you take it, Sly-One?'

'How can you say such a thing!' cried

Sly-One, pretending to be very angry.
'Go and ask the Ribbon-Woman, and
the Saucepan-Man, and the Balloon-
Man where I was this morning. They
will all tell you I was in their shops and
had nothing to do with your honey. But
let me tell you this – if anyone has stolen
it, I think it serves you right, for I
consider you're very mean indeed with
it!'

And with that, Sly-One stalked in at his front gate, feeling very fine indeed, for he thought he had played Sweet-Tooth a very clever trick.

'Well, I'll find that honey if I have to hunt for it myself!' called Sweet-Tooth. 'And if I find anyone eating honey, I'll just ask them how they came to have it!'

Now that made Sly-One feel rather uncomfortable. He knew what chatter-

boxes the elves were, and he was afraid they would hold a party, and tell everyone how they had bought a large pot of honey from Sly-One. Then Sweet-Tooth would be sure to hear about it.

'I'd better go to the elves and make them hide the honey for a little while until Sweet-Tooth has forgotten about it,' he decided. So off he went.

He soon arrived at the oak tree where the elves lived, and they told him how they had done just as he said and found the honey all ready for them.

'And we're going to hold a party this very afternoon, and have the honey then,' they shouted, as they came all round him. 'Here is the money, Sly-One, and thank you for letting us have the pot so cheaply.'

Sly-One took the money, and put it into his pocket.

'Listen to me,' he said. 'You must put off eating the honey for at least a week. It isn't ready yet. You'll make your-selves ill if you eat honey that's not ripe.'

'Not ripe!' cried the elves, in astonishment. 'We've never heard of honey that wasn't ripe before. But still, if it's as you say, we certainly won't eat it yet. What shall we do to ripen it?'

'You must dig a hole in the ground and bury it there,' said Sly-One. 'I'll come and tell you when it's ready to be eaten.'

So the elves dug a deep hole, and lowered the pot into it. Then they covered it with earth again, and ran back to their oak tree.

'Ha, ha!' said Sly-One to himself. 'Now everything's all right. I've got the money, and the honey is safely hidden away from Sweet-Tooth's sharp eyes.'

Now probably Sly-One would never have been found out if he hadn't been very greedy as well as sly. The more he thought of that honey safely buried away, the more he wished he could have a taste of it. And at last he made up his mind that he would, for the elves would never know.

So early one morning he set off to the

place where the pot was buried. He dug down to it, and came to the cover. He made a hole in it, and put his spoon through. Then he sipped the honey.

'My!' he said. 'Isn't it delicious!'

He went on and on sipping it – and then something happened. Sweet-Tooth, who had searched everywhere for her lost pot, and who had sent her servant out too, had at last told her bees to find it.

'Go and search through the woods and the fields,' she said. 'You are sure to find it somewhere. Then come back to me and tell me your news.'

It was that very morning that the bees started out. They flew buzzing all over the place, and you may be sure it wasn't long before they found Sly-One sitting by the hole sipping honey. Down they swooped, and buzzed all round him.

'Go away, go away!' he cried, waving his spoon. But they wouldn't. They settled on his hand, and he got up in a fright and ran away. They followed him, and when he caught his foot on a root and tumbled down, they flew down in a cloud, and soon you couldn't see Sly-One for bees!

'You're stinging me, you're stinging me!' he cried. But it wasn't any use shouting. The bees were angry, for they knew their mistress was in trouble, and they guessed Sly-One had taken their honey.

Well, in the end, there was nothing for Sly-One to do but to run all the way to Sweet-Tooth's house, and beg her to call off her bees. She did so, and then stared at him in surprise.

'What made them fasten on you like that?' she asked, severely.

'Honey,' sobbed Sly-One.

'Honey!' said Sweet-Tooth. 'Oho, so it was you that took my pot. Perhaps you'll tell me all about it now.'

So Sly-One told his story, crying with the pain of the bee-stings all the time. Sweet-Tooth listened with a frown.

'Do you want me to go to the king and queen and tell them this?' she asked. 'Oh, you don't? Well, listen to me. You're to go back to the green elves and tell them what you've done. Give them back their money and dig up that pot again. Bring it here to me, and I'll see how much damage you've done to it.'

So, weeping and sobbing, Sly-One did as he was told. How ashamed of him the elves were when he told them his story

and gave them back their money! How tired and hot Sly-One got, digging up the pot all by himself, for you may be sure no one would help him! He put it on his shoulder at last and carried it to Sweet-Tooth.

She peered into the pot.

'You have done a lot of damage to it,' she said. 'You had better pay me three pieces of silver.'

'I haven't got so many,' said Sly-One in despair.

'Very well, then, you must do some work for me instead,' said Sweet-Tooth. 'You shall come and chop firewood for me every day for a fortnight.'

And so he did, making everybody wonder at him, for it was well known that Sly-One never did a good turn to anyone.

'Well, it's the last time I ever play a mean trick on anyone again,' said the brownie, as he bound up his stings. 'It's not worth while!'

But whether he kept his word or not I have never heard!

5

Snippitty's Shears

Snippitty's garden was in a dreadful mess. The grass wanted cutting, the hedge wanted clipping, and the weeds had grown so tall that Snippitty could hardly see the flowers.

He had been away on his holiday, and he was very cross to see how untidy his garden was.

'I don't feel like spending all the week clipping and cutting,' he thought. 'I think I'll go to Puddle the gnome and buy a pair of magic shears. Then they can do the work, and I shall be able to sit in the sunshine and read my newspaper.'

So he went to Puddle's shop. It was a curious shop, hung with all kinds of things, from pins to balloons. Puddle was very clever, and he could put a spell into anything and make it very powerful indeed.

'I want a pair of shears with a cutting spell in them,' said Snippitty, when he walked inside the shop.

'Here's a fine pair,' said Puddle, taking down a glittering pair of sharp-looking shears.

'How much?' asked Snippitty.

'Thirty pence,' said Puddle.

'Don't be foolish,' said Snippitty. 'That's far too much.'

'It isn't, and you know it isn't,' said Puddle indignantly. 'Why, you couldn't buy these shears at even fifty pence in the next town. They would be quite seventy pence.'

Snippitty knew that that was true. Puddle's shears were very good indeed, and the magic in them made them powerful. But he was a mean little fellow, and he wasn't going to pay more

58

than he could help.

'I'll give you twenty pence for them,' he said, getting out his purse.

'No,' said Puddle.

'Yes,' said Snippitty. 'Not a penny more.'

'No, I tell you,' said Puddle. 'Why, they cost more than that to make.'

'I don't believe you,' said Snippitty, rudely.

Puddle looked at the mean little gnome and felt very angry.

'All right,' he said suddenly, with a grin. 'You can have them for twenty pence.'

Snippitty smiled in delight to think that he had got his way. He paid out the money, took the shears and went off with them.

He stuck them in the grass and said loudly: 'Shears, do your work!'

At once the shears began cutting the grass very closely and evenly. Snippitty watched them, pleased to think that he could sit down and read whilst his shears did all his work.

When the shears had finished cutting his lawn, Snippitty saw them fly across to the privet hedge and begin to clip that. He was delighted to see what a fine job they made of the hedge.

'I'll just finish this story in my paper and then set the shears to work on those tall weeds,' said Snippitty. So he settled down comfortably to his reading – but, dear me, his chair was so soft and the sun was so warm that Snippitty fell fast asleep!

He slept on and on – and the shears went on and on working. They finished the hedge and looked round for something else to clip. They flew across to the weeds and cut those down too. Then they clipped down all the rose trees that Snippitty was so proud of, and looked round for something else.

Clip! The clothes-line was cut in half and all the clothes fell to the ground. The shears soon cut them up into little pieces, and then looked round again.

Clip! Down came the tennis net, and was soon cut into tiny little pieces on the

Snippitty's Shears

lawn. What next? Ha, there was Snippitty lying fast asleep in the sunshine, his long white beard reaching almost down to his knees.

The shears flew over to him. Clip! Clip! Clip! The beard that Snippitty was so proud of was cut into three pieces, and the shears began to clip it very small. The noise woke Snippitty, and he sat up and yawned.

But, oh, my goodness, when he saw what the shears had done, he shouted in dismay.

'Stop! Stop! Oh, you wicked shears, look what you've done! You've taken off my beautiful beard! You've chopped my clothes-line in half! You've cut down my rose trees! You've ruined my tennis net! Oh, oh, stop, I tell you, stop!'

But nothing would stop those shears! They rushed at Snippitty and cut off the points of his shoes. Then they snipped all the buttons off his tunic and clipped the point off his hat. Snippitty gave a yell and rushed up the road to Puddle's shop. He burst in at the door and closed it behind him.

'Good gracious, Snippitty, whatever's the matter?' asked Puddle.

'It's those shears!' said Snippitty, almost crying. 'They've got a spell to make them work, but not one to make them stop. Put it in at once, Puddle. Look what they've done to my lovely beard!'

Puddle laughed till the tears rolled down his long nose and dropped on the counter with a splash.

'If you want another spell, it will be ten pence extra,' he said. 'I told you those shears were thirty pence, you know. You only paid me twenty pence and surely you didn't expect to get such a lot for your money. Will you pay me ten pence more, and I will put a stop-spell in the shears?'

Snippitty opened his purse and put ten pence on the counter.

'I have been mean,' he said. 'And I am well punished. Here is your money. Take it.'

Puddle took it, and then opened the door. The shears flew in and Puddle

64

chanted some magic words. In a trice the shears fell to the counter and lay there quite still.

Snippitty picked them up and shook them.

'You wicked things!' he cried. 'You've done pounds worth of damage! I'll put you in the dustbin!'

'Don't do that,' said Puddle. 'They might come in useful next year.'

'So they might,' said Snippitty with a sigh and put them under his arm. 'Well, I'm going back to clear up all the damage. Good-day to you, Puddle. I shan't be mean again. It certainly doesn't pay.'

And I quite agree with him, don't you?

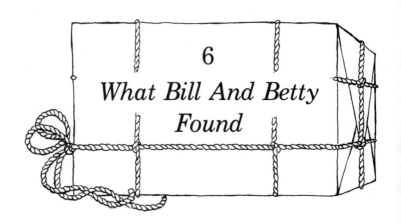

6

What Bill And Betty Found

Bill and Betty had just carried the clean washing to Mrs. Brown's house for their mother. It was a long way, and they were glad to come to the end of their journey, for the basket was heavy.

'Now for home and tea!' said Betty. So the two children ran down the road again, went through the village, and took the lane that ran up the hill to where their cottage stood.

Half-way up the lane they found a big parcel and they picked it up. It had no address on, and the children wondered whom it belonged to.

'I know!' said Bill. 'The carrier has dropped it off his cart. We'd better go right back to the village and give it to him. He always has tea at Mrs. Robinson's, and we shall catch him there!'

'But, Bill, the parcel is so heavy, and it's such a long way!' said poor Betty. 'I'm so tired and hungry.'

'Yes, but just think how worried someone will be if they don't get their parcel,' said Bill. 'No, Betty, we must go back, and ask the carrier if he has dropped it.'

So back they went, carrying the parcel. It took them half an hour to reach the village. They knocked at Mrs. Robinson's door, for they saw the carrier's cart standing outside, and knew that Jim the carrier must be inside.

'Please, does this parcel belong to Jim's cart?' asked Bill. Jim came running out to see.

'Yes, it does,' he said. 'I've got a label for it too, that must have dropped off it into the bottom of my cart. I was in a dreadful way when I found the label, for I felt certain that it must have belonged to a lost parcel. Well, you are good children!'

Jim fished in his pocket for the label

and tied it on. Then he looked closely at it, and smiled broadly.

'Who do you think the parcel is for?' he said. 'It's addressed to Miss Betty and Master Bill Smith, Hill Cottage, Brambletown.'

'Why, that's us!' cried Bill in surprise.

'Yes, it's you all right,' said Jim. 'Now aren't you glad you took the trouble to bring the parcel all the way back from where you found it? If you hadn't, someone else might have found it and kept it!'

'But fancy! A parcel for us!' said Betty. I wonder what can be in it?'

'We'll find out when we get home!' cried Bill. 'Come on, Betty, let's take it home now.'

'No, no, wait a minute,' said Jim. 'I've been very careless to drop that parcel like that. You wait just a moment and I'll take you all the way home in my cart.'

'Wait for twenty minutes,' said Mrs. Robinson, beaming at them, 'and have a cup of tea with me, my dears. I've got some of my new blackcurrant jam out and a fine chocolate cake made this afternoon. You come along and have some. I'm sure you must be hungry and tired, for I saw you pass a long time ago carrying a basket of washing.'

So Bill and Betty went in, and had a really delicious tea. Then Jim the carrier lifted them up beside him on the front seat of his cart, and clicked to his old horse. Off they all went down the road, Bill and Betty feeling as pleased as could be at getting such a lovely ride.

Mother was so astonished when she saw them arriving. The carrier explained everything, and said they were very good children. Then he lifted them down and they went indoors to undo the parcel.

Well, it was no wonder it was heavy! It was from their Auntie, and she had sent them simply lovely things.There was a great big doll for Betty with three changes of clothes. For Bill there were fifty soldiers, and a railway train. For Mother there was a beautiful red shawl, and for Daddy there were a hundred of his favourite cigarettes!

'Well, what a good thing we found that parcel and took it to the carrier!' said Bill. 'Nobody would have known who it was for, if we hadn't – and then we would never have got all our lovely

presents!'
'It was lucky!' said Betty.
And it certainly was, wasn't it?

7

The Adventurous Duck

Timothy had a bright new twenty pence that his uncle had given him to spend. So he went to the toy-shop on the sea-front to buy something with it. He chose a very fine floating duck, and ran with it down to the sea.

It floated beautifully. It bobbed up and down on the waves, and looked lovely. All the other boys and girls watched it and thought Timothy was very lucky.

But the duck was too adventurous. It floated out too far, and Timothy couldn't get it back again. On it went and on and on, right out to sea. Timothy watched it sadly, for it was a very beautiful duck.

Soon the duck was frightened. It couldn't see Timothy any more, and the sea was very large and deep. Fishes swam about underneath it, and great sea-gulls sailed overhead.

'I wish I hadn't been so adventurous,' said the duck, sadly. 'I wish I had kept close to Timothy. Now I shall be lost and never see him again.'

Suddenly the duck gave a frightened quack, and trembled all over its body. A big sea-gull was swooping nearer and nearer. At last it pounced on the little floating duck and picked it up in its yellow beak. Then away up in the air it flew, carrying the duck with it.

Higher and higher it went, and the other gulls came flying round to see what their friend held in his beak.

'Silly! Silly!' they cried. 'It's nothing to eat! It's just a stupid toy!'

The gull gave a screech, and dropped the duck again. Down it fell, and down and down. Then, far below, it saw a boat full of people. A little girl was in it, and she suddenly saw the falling duck. She held out her hands, and caught it just like a ball.

'Why, it's a dear little floating duck!' she cried in astonishment. 'Oh, I must take it out to tea with me this afternoon!'

So when she was rowed into shore, and trotted off to go to tea with her Auntie, she took the little duck with her. Her cousin was waiting for her at

the gate and she waved to him.

'Come and look what I've got!' she cried. 'It's a dear little floating duck that fell out of a gull's beak!'

Now who do you suppose her cousin was? Why, it was Timothy! He stared at the duck in surprise, for he could see that it was his.

'Why, that's the little duck I bought with the twenty pence your Daddy gave me this morning!' he said. It floated right away, and I saw a gull swoop down and pick it up!'

'And it dropped it into my hands!' cried the little girl. 'Oh, what an adventure it had, Timothy! Here it is, and I hope it will be a good duck now, and not go off by itself any more!'

Timothy took it in delight. He thought he had lost it for ever. He was pleased, and the little girl was pleased, and as for the floating duck, it was so full of joy that it couldn't even quack!

8

Ho-Ho's Bad Penny

Ho-Ho lived in Marigold Cottage, and was the meanest little gnome in the whole of Lemon village – but one day he got his punishment, as you shall hear.

He was digging in his garden one afternoon when his spade struck against something. He bent down to see what it was, and found that he had dug up a silver penny.

'Ho!' said Ho-Ho, rubbing it. 'What a find!'

But when he looked at it more closely, he saw that it was a bad silver penny, not worth so much as a farthing.

'What a pity!' he said. Then a naughty thought came into his head. 'Never mind, I'll give it to someone else and perhaps they won't notice!'

So that morning, when Binny the baker called with the bread, Ho-Ho paid his bill with the bad silver penny. Binny was short-sighted and he didn't see that it wasn't a good one. He popped it into his bag, said good-day to Ho-Ho and went off to his cart.

He drove off to his next customer, Loppy, the big black rabbit who lived in Sandy Burrow at the end of the village. Loppy didn't want any bread, but he asked Binny if he would like to see a beautiful barrow he had made that morning.

'My, that's a lovely one' said Binny, when he saw it. 'You are very clever with your paws, Loppy. I wish I had a barrow like that!'

'Would you like to buy this one?'

asked Loppy. 'I can easily make myself another.'

'How much is it?' asked Binny.

'A silver penny,' said Loppy.

'Well, here you are,' said Binny, and he slipped the bad silver penny that Ho-Ho had given him into Loppy's paw. Loppy put it into his pocket without looking at it.

'You can fetch the barrow tonight, when your work is done,' he told Binny. 'I'll have it all ready for you.'

Binny drove off again and Loppy went indoors. He put on his hat, took his stick and a basket and went out to do some shopping.

'I must get a new kettle!' he said to himself. 'My old one really won't last any longer!'

So he went up the street to where Tinkle kept a kettle and saucepan shop.

'Have you a nice big kettle?' asked Loppy. 'One with a good big handle?'

'Yes, Loppy,' said Tinkle, and took down a fat kettle with a big, curved handle. 'This is the best one I have in my shop.'

'How much is it?' asked Loppy.

'A silver penny,' said Tinkle.

'Very well, I'll have it,' said Loppy, and he gave Tinkle the bad silver penny. Tinkle popped it into the till, wrapped up the kettle and gave it to Loppy. Then another customer came in, and the little shopkeeper asked him what he wanted.

'Can you give me change for a gold penny?' asked the customer, a tall brownie with a long beard. 'I want to go in the bus and I am sure the conductor won't have any change.'

'Certainly,' said Tinkle. He opened the drawer of his till, and counted out ten silver pennies. The bad penny was among them, but he didn't notice it. The brownie gave him the gold penny, took the silver, said good-bye and ran to catch his bus. He hopped in, climbed up to the top, and sat down.

When he got home he unlocked the door of his little cottage, and found a note in his letter-box. He opened it and read it. It was from Wimple the pixie.

'I shall call for your rent this afternoon,' said the note. 'Please be sure to have it ready.'

'What a good thing I got change this morning!' said the brownie. 'I have plenty of silver pennies to pay the rent.'

He took two silver pennies from his pocket, put them in an envelope, wrote 'For Wimple the pixie' across it, and put in on his kitchen table. One of the two pennies was the bad one, though the brownie did not know it.

Not long after that there came a knock at the door, and the brownie opened it.

'Good afternoon,' said Wimple the pixie. 'Have you got my rent ready, Red-Coat?'

'Yes, here it is in this envelope,' said the brownie.

'Thank you,' said Wimple, and put it into his pocket without opening the envelope. He said good-bye and ran off.

When he got home he looked at his garden. It was dreadfully untidy.

'I really must have my garden dug up,' he said to himself.'It's a perfect disgrace. I'll send a note to Ho-Ho the gnome, and ask him to come along to-morrow and do a day's work in it. He's a good gardener and I'm sure it will look better when he has worked in it for a while.'

So he wrote a note to Ho-Ho, and sent his little servant down the road with it. She came back with a message to say that Ho-Ho would be along the next day at eight o'clock in the morning, with his spade and fork.

Next morning Ho-Ho turned up, and began to dig hard. Wimple's garden was not very big, and Ho-Ho soon managed to make it neat and tidy. When five o'clock came Wimple gave him some tea, and asked him how much he would charge him for his day's work.

'A silver penny,' said Ho-Ho.

'Here you are,' said Wimple, and gave him one of the two pennies he had had from Red-Coat the brownie. Ho-Ho put it into his pocket without looking at it.

'Good-bye,' he said. 'I must be getting home.'

He set off down the street, but on the way he thought he would buy a meat-pie for his supper. So he stopped at Mother Puff's and looked in at the window. Then he put his hand in his pocket to see what money he had got. He had two farthings and the silver penny that Wimple had given him. Ho-Ho looked at it.

Then he frowned angrily.

'Why, if it isn't a bad one!' he cried. 'The wicked pixie, to give me a bad silver penny! I shall go to Mr. Dumps the policeman, and tell him all about it!'

He went to Mr. Dumps's house and banged on the door. When the policeman came, Ho-Ho showed him the bad silver penny.

'Dear, dear!' said Mr. Dumps, looking worried. 'We can't have this sort of thing! Where did you get it from, Ho-Ho?'

'Wimple gave it to me,' said Ho-Ho.

'Well, I must go along and ask him about it,' said Mr. Dumps. So Ho-Ho and Mr. Dumps walked down the street to Wimple's house. The pixie was most surprised to see them, and when he heard what they had come about, he went quite white.

'I didn't know it was a bad silver penny,' he said in a shaking voice. 'It was one of two silver pennies that I got from Red-Coat the brownie for his rent yesterday.'

'Well, we'll go along to him, then!' said Mr. Dumps the policeman. So they all went to Red-Coat's house, and asked him how he had managed to give Wimple a bad silver penny.

'Well, I didn't know it was bad!' said Red-Coat, looking worried. 'It was one of ten that I got from Tinkle's yesterday when he gave me change for a gold piece.'

'We'll go along and ask Tinkle about it,' said Mr. Dumps. So he and Ho-Ho, Wimple and Red-Coat all went to Tinkle's kettle shop.

Tinkle was most surprised to see them all, and still more surprised when he heard what they had come about.

'Well, let me think,' he said. 'I had nine good silver pennies yesterday, I know, because I counted them in the morning before I opened my shop, and I know they were good ones because I looked at all of them. Now, where did I get the tenth? Oh, I know! Loppy the rabbit gave it to me when he bought a big kettle.'

'Well go along and see Loppy then!' said Mr. Dumps. So they all went along to Sandy Burrow and knocked on Loppy's door.

Loppy listened to Mr. Dumps's story, and pulled his whiskers as he thought where he had got the silver penny from.

'Binny the baker gave it to me when he bought a barrow from me,' he said. 'I hadn't any other silver penny, so it must have been the one he gave me.'

Ho-Ho's Bad Penny

'Well, we'll go along to Binny's,' said Mr. Dumps. So they all trotted down the street to Binny's cottage. He was sitting in his front garden, reading a newspaper.

'What do you all want?' he asked. Mr. Dumps told him, and Binny scratched his head and thought.

'Oh, I know who gave me the silver penny!' he said, and he pointed straight at Ho-Ho the gnome, who was looking very uncomfortable indeed, and wishing to goodness he had never gone to Mr. Dumps at all. 'It was Ho-Ho himself, so it was! He was the only one who paid his bread bill yesterday, and he gave me a silver penny. It must have been the bad one.'

Everyone turned and stared at Ho-Ho. He went as red as a beetroot, and hung his head down.

'WHERE DID YOU GET THAT BAD SILVER PENNY? said Mr. Dumps, in a very stern voice.

'I d-d-d-dug it out of my g-g-g-garden!' said Ho-Ho.

'Oh, you did, did you?' said Mr. Dumps. 'Well, I suppose, when you came to me to complain that Wimple had given you a bad penny, you wanted me to spank him for doing such a naughty thing. Now we find it is you who sent this penny all round the village, so you must be spanked. Come here!'

Then Ho-Ho was spanked by the policeman, and all the others gave him one spank too. He ran home to Marigold Cottage crying all the way.

'What a wicked gnome I've been!' he sobbed. 'I've got to pay Binny's bill again, and I've done a whole day's work for Wimple for nothing, for I daren't ask him to give me a good silver penny now, and Mr. Dumps has got the bad one. Oh, I'll never, never be able to hold up my head in Lemon Village again! I'd better pack up and go.'

He put all his clothes into a bag, caught the next bus out of Fairyland, and went to live on the moon. Nobody has ever heard of him since, but Mr. Dumps has still got the bad silver penny. He keeps it in a box, together with a burglar's lantern, a pearl whose owner was never found, and a book all about finger-prints. He'll show it to you, if ever you call at his house.

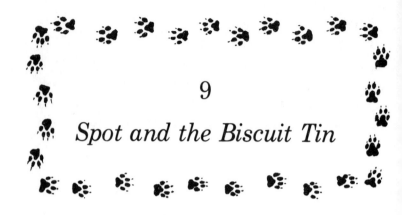

9

Spot and the Biscuit Tin

Spot was a little brown and white dog. He belonged to Timothy and Judy, and he loved his little master and mistress very much. He sat up with his two ears cocked to listen to what they were saying.

'It's Baby's birthday tomorrow,' Judy said. 'I'd forgotten all about it. What shall we buy her, Timmy?'

'Let's look in our money-box and see how much we've got,' said Timmy. So they took down the pig that held their pennies and unscrewed its head. Out fell two pennies and one twopence piece.

'Ooh, only four pence!' said Timmy, in surprise. 'How's that, Judy?'

'Oh, don't you remember, we took a whole five pence out last week to buy some flowers for that ill old woman,' said Judy. 'Oh dear! four pence won't buy Baby very much, will it – and I did so want to get her one of those soft cuddly bunnies in the toy-shop. I know she would love that.'

Just then Mummy came into the room and looked at the children with a smile.

'Counting your money?' she said. 'Well, how much have you got for Baby's birthday?'

'Only four pence!' said Judy, sadly. 'I do wish it was lots more, Mummy. How can we get any more?'

'You'd better try and find old Mr. Giles' spoons and forks!' said Mummy, with a laugh. 'They were stolen from his house last night, and the burglars must have packed them in a biscuit tin, for they had emptied the biscuits on the table, and the tin was gone. The burglars were caught, but they had buried the tin somewhere and won't say where. Whoever can find it will get a reward.'

'Oh, wouldn't it be lovely if we could find it!' said Judy in excitement. 'But

I'm sure we can't.'

Spot, the little dog, was listening hard to everything that was said. As soon as he heard about the biscuit tin, he wagged his tail. He knew what a biscuit tin was, and he knew the smell of it, too. He would try to find it for them!

He licked Judy's hand and tugged at her skirt.

'I do believe Spot wants to go and find the spoons and forks!' said Judy, with a laugh. 'Well, we'll all go. Come on, Timmy.'

All morning the two children and the dog hunted everywhere to find where the biscuit tin could have been buried. They looked under hedges, they looked in ditches. They went across the fields and looked everywhere to see if they could find a place where the earth had been newly dug.

But they couldn't. There just didn't seem anywhere that was likely. Soon it was dinner-time and the two children were tired out.

'Let's go home,' said Judy, with a sigh. 'We can't find those spoons and forks, Timmy. Perhaps nobody will, and when the two burglars come out of prison, they'll go and get them, and poor Mr. Giles will never see them again. What a pity!'

Spot listened. He watched the children turn towards home, but he didn't go with them. No, he had an idea of his own. He would go and hunt whilst they were having dinner. He had thought of a very good place.

As soon as the children were out of sight Spot ran off. He went to where a great pit had been dug out of the hillside for gravel, and began to search there. It was a place that no one ever went to, for it was far from the lane, and quite deserted.

Spot sniffed here and he sniffed there. His sharp little nose went under the prickly gorse bushes, and into the blackberry brambles. He sniffed in this rabbit hole and in that, but for a long time it wasn't a bit of good.

'I shall have to give up,' said Spot. 'I'm feeling very hungry.'

Just as he turned to go, a smell came to his nose. It was very faint, but Spot knew what it was. Biscuits!

'Now there can't be any biscuits here, so it must be the hidden biscuit tin I can smell!' thought Spot, excitedly. 'I will find where this smell comes from.'

He sniffed hard, and then ran in the direction of the smell. It seemed to come from under a pile of stones. Spot ran to them. Yes, the smell certainly lay under the stones. Perhaps the burglars buried the tin of spoons and forks in the ground, and then piled stones on top to hide the newly turned earth.

The stones were big, but Spot managed to scratch them away. The biscuit smell was stronger than ever. He began to dig excitedly in the earth with his strong little paws.

Ah, what was that? His paws struck against something hard. Yes, it was a biscuit tin! – Hurrah!

But Spot couldn't get the tin out of the earth, however much he tried. So off he ran to fetch Timmy and Judy. When he got home he tugged at Timmy's trousers, and the little boy guessed that he wanted him to follow where he led. So he and Judy set off after Spot.

When they came to where the biscuit tin was half dug up, how astonished they were! They opened the lid and there, neatly packed inside, were all Mr. Giles' silver spoons and forks!

'Oh, you clever, clever little dog!' cried the children. 'Come on, we'll take them to Mr. Giles and get the reward!'

Off they went, carrying the tin, and Mr. Giles was most delighted to see them. He was very much astonished to hear how clever Spot had been.

'Here is the reward,' he said. And what do you think it was? A whole five pounds!

'Ooh!' cried the children in delight. 'What a lovely present we can buy for Baby's birthday tomorrow! And something for clever little Spot too!'

They ran to the shops and bought Baby a lovely cuddly bunny with big ears and a little white bob-tail. Then they looked at Spot.

'We've got three pounds left,' they told him. 'What would you like for yourself?'

Spot chose a wonderful collar with tiny bells on, and a bar of chocolate. He marched home with his new collar outside and his chocolate inside! And when the other dogs met him and asked him why he had such a fine new collar on, wasn't he proud to tell them!

10

The Sailor Doll goes to Sea

Jack, the sailor doll, was very vain. He was dressed in a sailor's uniform, and he thought he looked very grand indeed.

'I'm the finest toy in the nursery!' he said. 'I can dance the horn-pipe and whistle it too!'

'Pooh!' said the panda. 'You call yourself a sailor doll and yet you've never been to sea! You're a fraud!'

The sailor doll went red. All the toys laughed at him.

'Ha, you're as vain as can be, and yet you've never been to sea!'

'Well, I will go to sea, so there!' said the sailor doll, angrily. 'I'm brave enough for anything. I'll go to sea this very day, and then you'll never see me again! And you'll be sorry then.'

The sailor doll frowned hard at the laughing toys. Then he marched to the nursery door.

'What are you going to sea in?' cried the panda. 'What about this wooden boat? Wouldn't that do?'

'All right,' said the sailor doll, looking at the toy boat. 'But it's too big for me to carry by myself till I come to the sea.'

'We'll all help you,' said the panda. So the teddy bear, the panda, the wooden soldiers, the talking doll and all the other toys helped the sailor doll to take the toy boat out of the nursery.

They walked down the garden and out into the lane. Then they began to look for the sea.

'Hi! Look! There's the sea!' cried the panda suddenly, pointing to the duck-pond. 'Hurrah! We've found it! My word, isn't it big?'

The sailor doll began to tremble when he saw all the water; but he didn't dare to show that he was frightened. He walked along with the others and came to the water-side. The panda and the teddy placed the toy boat on the water, and the sailor doll got in.

'Well, I'm off to sea,' he said. 'Good-bye, everyone. Perhaps you're sorry, now that I'm really off!'

He shook hands with each one of them and then the panda pushed the boat off into the water. It bobbed away, and the sailor doll clutched the sides in fright. He had no oars, and he wouldn't have known how to use them if he had. He hoped and hoped his boat wouldn't upset.

'Good-bye, good-bye!' shouted the toys, waving their hands. 'Perhaps we'll see you again some day.'

The sailor doll drifted out into the middle of the pond where the white ducks were. He was very much afraid of the big, quacking creatures. One of them pecked at his boat and set it swaying to and fro. The sailor doll was afraid it would upset.

'Go away, you wicked creature!' he cried fiercely to the duck. 'Go away!'

The ducks were surprised and frightened. They swam away. The sailor doll was pleased to find that they thought

him so fierce. His boat floated on and on, bobbing up and down on the ripples left by the white ducks.

Suddenly a large, green frog popped its nose out of the water and looked at him. Then it took hold of the side of the boat with one of its feet and began to climb in.

The sailor doll hung on to the swaying boat and looked at the frog in fright. Then he had a grand idea.

'Get away, or I'll call the ducks here and they'll eat you!' he said. The frog gave a frightened croak and slipped back into the water at once. The sailor doll sat up and watched him swim away.

'Ha, I'm a brave doll!' he thought. 'If only the other toys could have seen all these adventures!'

But his adventures were not over yet. Oh dear me, no! A fish suddenly jumped right out of the water after a fly, and fell into the sailor doll's boat. It was a stickleback, and the doll was very much afraid of its seven spines.

'Catch me by the tail and throw me back!' begged the struggling fish. 'I shall die if you don't.'

The sailor doll caught him by the tail and with a jerk threw him overboard. The fish was very grateful and popped its nose out to thank him.

'Is there any way in which I can help you?' it said.

'Could you bump my boat along with your nose?' asked the doll. 'It seems to have stopped in the middle of the sea, and I want to get on with my travels.'

'Certainly,' said the fish, and it gave the boat a hard bump. But, oh dear, it bumped so suddenly that the boat turned upside down and the sailor doll was thrown out into the water! The fish swam up to him and begged him to get astride his back.

'Thank you,' said the sailor doll, shivering and shaking with the wet and cold. 'Take me to land, please. I'm tired of the sea.'

The fish swam with him right across the pond and put him down on the opposite side. The sailor doll thought that he had crossed the sea to another land. He sat down in the sun and dried himself.

'I wish I hadn't left home,' he sighed. 'Here I am far away across the sea in a strange land, and I shall never see my friends any more. If only I were home with them I would never be vain or silly again.'

After a while he got up and started to walk by the edge of the pond. He went on and on and on, thinking sadly of all the toys he had left behind.

And they were thinking of him and feeling very sorry they had laughed at him and made him go to sea, because really they were quite fond of him, though they got tired of him when he was silly.

'Oh dear, what a shame that we sent him away to sea,' sighed the panda. 'I do hope he won't come to any harm.'

'Let's go down to the sea again and see if we can see him anywhere,' said the talking doll. So off they all went. But, of course, there was nothing to be seen on the water except the white ducks.

The sailor doll walked and walked by the edge of the water. The pond was a round one, and soon he had walked so far that he had nearly reached the place where he had set sail in his boat that morning!

And suddenly all the toys saw him coming along! They could hardly believe their eyes.

'Why, there he is!' they cried. 'Hip-hip-hurrah!'

The sailor doll heard them cheering and looked at them in astonishment.

'Goodness!' he said. 'How did you get here? Why, I've been right across the sea to the other side, and when I got to the strange land there I began to walk and walk and now – here we all are!'

'This is where we said good-bye to you this morning,' said the panda, and they couldn't understand how it all happened.

'Well, never mind,' said the sailor doll happily. 'I'm so glad to be back. Are you glad to see me, toys?'

'Oh, yes!' cried everyone. 'We're sorry we made you go away.'

'And I'm sorry I used to be so silly,' said the sailor doll. 'But I've been to sea now, haven't I, so I'm a real, proper sailor!'

'Yes!' cried the panda. 'Come on, we'll all go home, and when we're safely there we'll hear you tell your adventures!'

So home they all went, very proud indeed of the sailor doll who had been to sea, visited a strange country and came back safe home again – and do you know, none of them ever guessed that he had only been to the other side of the little round duck-pond.

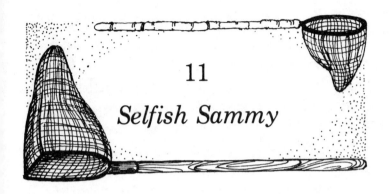

11

Selfish Sammy

Millie and James were staying with their Cousin Sammy. They didn't like him a bit. He wouldn't let them play with his best toys, and he wouldn't even let them read one of his books unless he held it - and it is most uncomfortable to read a book that someone else is holding.

He was a greedy boy too. He liked to have the biggest slice of cake, the biggest piece of pudding and the bun with the most sugar on. Millie and James were much too polite to tell him that his manners were very bad, but they began to wish that it was time to go home.

Sammy lived by the seaside, and it was quite a treat for Millie and James to stay with their Auntie Mary, Uncle Hugh and Grandpa. They could build sand castles, paddle, go shrimping and bathe. If only Sammy had been a nice cousin they would have been very happy – but he really was horrid.

One day Grandpa said they could all go prawning down on the rocks, because the tide would be out very far that day.

'I'll buy you each a prawning-net,' he said. 'And I'll give two prizes – one for the biggest prawn brought home, and one for the boy or girl who brings the most prawns home. Cook shall boil them for tea, so mind you catch a nice lot!'

The children were very excited. Grandpa always gave such nice prizes – and how kind of him to buy prawning-nets! They all set off to the toy-shop together with the money he had given them.

Sammy had the money in his pocket. It was sixty pence. At the shop there were two or three different nets, some cheaper than others – and what do you think that selfish Sammy did? Why, he bought a fine big net for himself, strong and well-made, and two small, silly little nets for Millie and James!

'I don't mind having a little net myself,' said James, 'but I do think you might be polite enough to let Millie have a nice one, Sammy.'

'I'm sure Grandpa meant you to spend twenty pence on each of us,' said Millie.

'I'm the oldest, so I must have the best,' said Sammy.

'You're only three days older than I am,' said James. 'I think you're mean.'

'Well, that's not the way to talk to someone you've come to stay with,' said Sammy. 'When you go out to stay, you have to be polite.'

'And when you have people to stay with you, you're supposed to be polite to them!' said James, angrily.

'Oh, don't let's quarrel,' said Millie. 'We're wasting time.'

'Well, but Sammy will be sure to catch the most prawns in his lovely big net,' said James. 'It isn't fair – we've only got small ones.'

'We might catch the biggest prawn, though, and there's a prize for that too,' said Millie. 'Come on, James; don't take any notice of Sammy. We'll catch the biggest prawn, you'll see!'

But wasn't it a pity – they didn't! At least, James did catch the biggest one – a real beauty – but five minutes later Sammy caught a monster. You should have seen his whiskers! So James's biggest prawn became the second biggest. He was so disappointed.

Sammy caught a tremendous lot of prawns. His net came up with dozens in, and he counted them carefully when he put them into his bag. Millie caught twenty-two, and James caught twenty. All Millie's prawns were rather small. She had no big ones at all.

'It looks as if Sammy will get both prizes!' said Millie to James.

'Never mind!' whispered back James. 'I'd rather have no prize at all than get one by cheating! His net can catch lots more than ours!'

At tea time Grandpa came out on the steps of the house and rang the tea bell to call them home.

'Hurry up!' called Sammy, pulling up his net for the last time. 'It's time to go! My, what a lot I've got! Fifty-seven! I shall get both prizes! Hurray!'

Millie and James said nothing. They put their bags round their shoulders and began to step across the rocks to go home. Sammy was in such a hurry to get to Grandpa and show him all his prawns that he began to jump from one rock to another, instead of going carefully.

'Look out!' cried James. 'You'll slip if you go so quickly, Sammy.'

'Pooh!' said Sammy, scornfully. 'I live at the seaside all the year round, and you don't. I'm good at jumping over rocks.'

But even as he spoke, his foot slipped on some seaweed, and splash! He slipped right into a deep rockpool, almost up to his shoulders!

'Help, help!' he screamed. Millie and James ran to him as fast as they could and pulled him out. How wet he was! And how frightened!

And oh, dear me, he had spilt every
single prawn out of his bag! Yes, every
one! What do you think of that? They
had all fallen into the water, and were
nowhere to be seen.

'Boo-hoo-hoo!' wept Sammy, who was a dreadful coward. 'I was nearly drowned, and all my prawns are gone.'

They all went home, Sammy still crying loudly. Grandpa came out to see what was the matter.

'Good gracious, you don't mean to say you are making all that noise, simply because you fell into a pool!' he said. 'Don't be silly, Sammy. I'm ashamed of you.'

'I've s-s-s-spilt all my p-p-prawns,' wept Sammy. 'And I had the most and the biggest too.'

'Go in and get some dry things on, and then come to me again,' said Grandpa. 'And STOP MAKING THAT NOISE!'

James and Millie went in to wash their hands, and Sammy went to change his clothes. Grandpa sat down on the balcony. He looked at the three prawning-nets. When he saw that one was much bigger and better than the others, he was astonished. He frowned very hard.

'That's not fair,' he said. 'But perhaps the two boys let Millie have a bigger one. That would be very nice of them.'

When all three came out to him, wondering what the prizes were, he looked at Millie.

'I suppose you had the biggest net, my dear,' he said.

'No, Grandpa, this is mine,' said Millie, showing him a small one. 'The big one belongs to Sammy.'

'Do you really mean to say that you were selfish enough to buy yourself that big net and get the others those small ones?' said Grandpa to Sammy. Sammy went very red and hung his head.

'Well, I think it was a very good punishment for you, to slip into that pool and lose all your prawns,' said Grandpa, sternly. 'Now then, which of you two, Millie and James, caught the biggest prawn, and the most?'

'Grandpa, I caught the biggest prawn and I caught the most too!' said Sammy. 'I lost them all, but I have won the prizes really.'

'I said the prizes would go to the ones who brought home the biggest prawn and the most,' said Grandpa. 'You didn't bring yours home; you dropped them in the pool. And I think it was a very good thing you did, you mean, selfish little boy! Even if you had brought them home, you wouldn't have won the prizes fairly, because you bought yourself the best net. I'm ashamed of you. Go indoors and don't let me see you again this evening!'

'Boo-hoo-ho!' wept Sammy, going indoors.

'And STOP THAT NOISE!' called Grandpa. Sammy stopped it – he knew that Grandpa would spank him if he didn't.

James got one prize for catching the biggest prawn, and Millie got one for catching the most. James's prize was a fine sailing-boat, and Millie's was a new spade. They were so pleased.

'Sammy, Sammy!' called James. 'Come and help me to sail my new ship! don't cry any more – we'll be friends!'

Sammy came out, wiping his eyes. He looked very much ashamed of himself.

'I'm very sorry I was mean,' he said. 'I won't be selfish any more, if you really will be friends with me. I know I was horrid.'

'Well, you were!' said Millie. 'But we'll forget it! Let's have tea and then go out and sail James's new ship!'

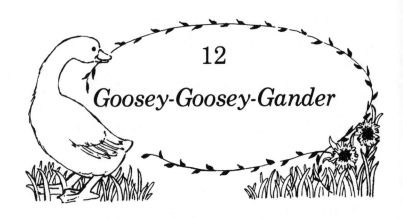

12
Goosey-Goosey-Gander

There was once a large grey gander who belonged to Mrs. Tubby and her husband. He was very clever and, really, he almost understood what Mrs. Tubby used to say to him each day.

'Goosey-gander follows me about like a dog,' said Mrs. Tubby, proudly. 'And see, husband, he can shut the gate with his beak just as easily as I shut it with my hand!'

Sure enough the goose could shut the gate. He had watched Mrs. Tubby shut the field-gate every day, and he knew exactly how to slip the catch in its place. He really was a very clever bird.

Mr. Tubby was a shepherd, and looked after the sheep and the lambs on Farmer Giles' hillside. He hadn't very much money, but he grew potatoes and cabbages in his little garden, and they made quite good soup when Mrs. Tubby had cooked them in her own special way.

One day Mrs. Tubby slipped on the kitchen floor and twisted her ankle. Mr. Tubby fetched the doctor, and he shook his head gravely.

'Dear, dear!' he said. 'This is serious, Mrs. Tubby. You will have to go to bed until your ankle is better. I will come and see you every day.'

Poor Mrs. Tubby! There was such a
lot to do in the cottage and only her to
do it, for Mr. Tubby was minding sheep
all day. He wondered how they were
going to manage, and then he went to
fetch his little niece, Mary. She was
only nine years old, but she was a very
useful little girl.

'Yes, Uncle Tubby,' she said, 'I will
come and look after Aunt Tubby till
she is well. I can cook dinner and I can

do housework. Don't worry.'

So Mr. Tubby didn't worry any more, but left things to Mary. She made the beds, washed up, cooked and scrubbed, and was the most useful little girl in the world. She fed Goosey-gander too, and he was very fond of her. She always left him to shut the gate of the sheep field when she took Uncle Tubby his dinner, and he never forgot.

When Mrs. Tubby was better, and Mary had gone back home, Mr. Tubby began to worry about the doctor's bill.

'How can we pay it?' he said. 'It isn't much, it's true, because he's only charged us about a pound a visit but I haven't any money put by, wife.'

'We must sell the old Goosey-gander,' said Mrs. Tubby. 'He's the only thing we've got that will fetch money.'

'Well, I'll be sorry to part with him,' said Mr. Tubby, with a sigh. 'He's a good bird, and great company. He often comes and sits with me when I'm minding my sheep. Still, the doctor's bill must be paid, so he must go.'

Poor Goosey-gander! He was very much upset when Mrs. Tubby told him he was to go to market and be sold. He was afraid that he might be fattened up and eaten for somebody's Christmas dinner. He worried about it so much that it kept him awake at night.

One moonlight night when Goosey-gander was sitting on one leg in the little shed, wide awake and sad, he heard a noise. He waddled to the door and looked out. The moon was up and shone down brightly. Goosey-gander looked up the hillside, trying to see if the sheep and lambs were safe.

And what did he see but a dark figure going in at the sheep-field gate! It wasn't Mr. Tubby, because Goosey-gander could hear him snoring in the cottage. It wasn't Farmer Giles, because he was big and fat, and this figure was lean and small.

It was the poacher, Jim Hookey! The farmer had driven him away the week before, and told him he would put him in prison if he caught any more hares on his land, and Jim had said he would pay back the farmer somehow. Now he was going to open the field-gate and drive out the lambs and the sheep so that they would all be scattered about and lost by the next morning.

Goosey-gander gave a loud hiss of rage. He was very fond of his master and he didn't like to think of how angry the farmer might be with Mr. Tubby if he found all his sheep and lambs strayed from the field. He would think that Mr. Tubby had forgotten to shut the gate.

'Ss-ss-ss-ss-ss-ss-ss-ss!' hissed Goosey-gander and waddled out of the shed. He

walked to the field-gate and looked about for the poacher. He was driving the sheep and the lambs towards the open gate. Goosey-gander chuckled to himself and hid in the hedge. Just as the sheep and lambs came running up, he flew out with great wings flapping, and cackled at the top of his voice:

'Cackle, cackle, cackle, cackle,cackle, cackle!'

The sheep stopped in fright, and ran right away up the field again. The poacher stopped in fright too, and the gander flew right at him and flapped his strong wings in his face.

'Ooooh!' cried the poacher, terrified, and he ran helter-skelter out of the gate and rushed down the lane as fast as his legs could carry him. He thought the gander was an old witch.

Goosey-gander watched him go. He was very pleased. He saw that all the sheep were safely at the other end of the field, and then he waddled to the gate. He shut it carefully and then put the catch in place with his beak.

He turned to go back to his shed, when he saw a big fat man watching him. It was Farmer Giles. Goosey-gander liked him, so he said: 'Cackle! cackle!' very softly and rubbed his head against him.

'Well, Goosey-gander, I saw all you did!' said Farmer Giles. 'You're the cleverest bird I've ever seen! I saw you turn back the sheep, frighten the poacher, and shut the gate. Well, you've saved me a lot of trouble and loss, and I'll tell your master in the morning what a fine bird you are!'

Goosey-gander waddled back home to his shed and went to sleep. In the morning he went to knock on the door to waken Mr. Tubby, as he always did.

Farmer Giles came down to see Mr. Tubby after breakfast, and was just in time to catch Mrs. Tubby going off to market with Goosey-gander. She had meant to sell him that very day.

'Where are you taking that goose to?' asked Farmer Giles.

'To sell him at the market, to pay our

doctor's bill,' answered Mrs. Tubby. 'Poor bird, we're very fond of him, but he's the only thing we've got to sell.'

'Well, let me tell you what I saw him doing last night,' said the farmer, and he told Mrs. Tubby all he had seen. She was most astonished, and called Mr. Tubby from the sheep-field to tell him all about it.

'You mustn't sell a clever gander like that,' said the farmer. 'I'll pay your doctor's bill for you, and you shall keep him. He saved my sheep for me, and I'd like to do something for him in return. I'm sure he'd like to stay with you instead of being sold.'

Goosey-gander was overjoyed! He flew at the farmer in delight and almost knocked him over.

'Cackle, cackle, cackle!' he cried. 'Cackle, cackle, cackle!'

He still lives with Mr. and Mrs. Tubby, and is very happy. Every Christmas Farmer Giles sends him a present, and what do you think it is? A big tin of peas! He simply loves to eat them, and all the time he hisses happily – like this: 'Ss-ss-ss-ss-ss-ss-ss!'

13

The Rabbit's Whiskers

Mr. Woffles was a large toy rabbit, and he lived in a nice little house in Toyland. He had fine whiskers, and he was very, very proud of them.

Now one day he went to the hair-dresser and asked for a hair cut. The hairs on his ears were really getting rather long, and as he wanted to go to a party at the teddy-bear's that evening he wanted to look smart.

The hairdresser was a wooden doll with black hair painted on his head so that it looked very neat and smooth. He took up his scissors and began to snip.

Snip,snap,snip,snap! went his scissors. Some of the hairs went into Mr. Woffle's eyes, and he shut them tight. When he opened them again, oh my goodness, what a shock he got!

The hairdresser had cut off all his fine whiskers!

'Ooh!' shouted Mr. Woffles, in dismay. 'I say! Why did you cut off my whiskers? Just look at that! Oh my, I do look a fright.'

'Sorry, sir, but you didn't say I wasn't to,' said the hairdresser.

'I didn't say you were to, either!' groaned the poor rabbit. 'Now what am I to do? No rabbit goes out without whiskers, not even a toy rabbit like me. And I'm to go to a party tonight!'

He went groaning out of the hairdresser's and quite forgot to pay his bill. The hairdresser didn't like to remind him because he felt very sorry to have made such a dreadful mistake about the whiskers.

Mr. Woffles felt so bad that he turned quite pale, and when he met his friends, Mrs. Plush Duck and Mr. Sailor Doll, they wondered what was the matter.

'Don't you feel well?' they asked. 'And oh - what's happened to your fine whiskers?'

Then Mr. Woffles told them, and they were just as upset as he was.

'Never mind,' said Mrs. Plush Duck, thinking hard. 'Come with me to the gooseberry bed. Gooseberries grow whiskers, you know, and maybe we can get some from them for you.'

So they all went to the gooseberry bushes and had a look at the gooseberries.

'Well, they certainly grow whiskers,' said Mr. Woffles the rabbit, looking at the hairy gooseberries. 'But they are such little ones. They wouldn't be any use to me.'

'No, they wouldn't,' agreed Mr. Sailor Doll. 'Well, let's think of something else.'

So they thought and thought, and then Mr. Sailor Doll remembered that he had seen a lot of whiskery-looking things lying in the pine wood not very far away.

'The pine trees drop them,' he said. 'They are long and brown, and might do quite well for you, Mr. Woffles.'

'Oh, do you mean the pine needles?' asked Mrs. Plush Duck. 'Yes, they might do. Let's go and see.'

'I don't think I should very much like to wear pine needles,' said Mr. Woffles. 'They sound rather sharp to me.'

'Just come and see them,' said his friends. 'They lie about under the trees in hundreds.'

So they went to the pine woods, and picked up a great many pine needles. They stuck them into Mr. Woffles' cheeks, and he didn't like them at all. 'No,' he said, firmly; 'They won't do. They're too stiff, and they hurt me, and they look silly. We must think of something else.'

So they threw them away, and tried hard to think of another idea. They were sitting there thinking when who should come along but Blackie, the lovely spaniel dog that lived just outside

Toyland. He was very friendly with Old Mother Hubbard who lived not far away, and often used to come to see her.

'What's the matter?' he asked the three toys, seeing them sitting so sadly together.

'The hairdresser stupidly cut off my whiskers this morning,' said Mr. Woffles. 'We are trying to think of where I can get some new ones to wear at the teddy-bear's party tonight. We've looked at the gooseberry whiskers, but they're too small. And we've tried these pine needle whiskers and they're too sharp and stiff.'

Blackie sat down and scratched his silky head. 'Let me see –' he said, and just then Mrs. Plush Duck cried out in excitement:

'Look!' she said. 'You've scratched out a lot of lovely long silky hairs from your head! Mr. Woffles, surely those would make fine whiskers for you!'

Mr. Woffles picked up the hairs that had fallen from Blackie's coat and tried them against his cheeks.

'How do they look?' he asked.

'Fine!' said everyone. 'They show up well against your sandy cheeks.'

'Let's go to the Toy Hospital and get them stuck on for you,' said Mrs. Plush Duck. So Blackie, Mr. Woffles, Mr. Sailor Doll and Mrs. Plush Duck all went to the Toy Hospital, where broken dolls were mended, wheels put on carts, and stitches put into toy animals whose sawdust was leaking out.

The toy doctor took a brush full of glue and dotted little specks of it over Mr. Woffles's cheeks. Then he lightly stuck the black hairs into the dots of glue.

'They will be dried hard in ten minutes,' he said. 'Then they will be quite all right.'

And in ten minutes, sure enough, the dots of glue were hard, and dear me, Mr. Woffles' new whiskers looked very grand indeed. They stuck out from his cheeks and were much longer than the ones he had had before.

'I'm much obliged to you for letting

me have your long hairs,' he said to
Blackie.

'Oh, I'm very pleased about it,' said Blackie. 'You do look fine! Everyone at the party will wonder where you got such fine whiskers from!'

And so they did – even the stuffed tiger, whose whiskers were longer than any other toy's, kept looking and looking at Mr. Woffles. He had a lovely time, and when he saw that the wooden hairdresser hadn't anyone to dance with, he forgave him for cutting off his whiskers and went to ask him if he would like a dance.

That was really very nice of him, wasn't it?

14

Angelina Jane

There was once a very beautiful doll
called Angelina Jane. She had bright
golden curly hair, shining blue eyes, a
rosebud mouth, and the loveliest pink
silk dress and bonnet that you can
imagine. She lived in Mollie's nursery
and she was very proud of herself
indeed.

She gave herself many airs and
graces and was so vain and selfish that
none of the toys liked her. Angelina
wanted them to make her queen of the
nursery, but they wouldn't.

'You're too vain!' they said. 'Go away, Jane, and don't think of yourself so much!'

'You're *not* to call me Jane!' said the doll angrily. 'My name is Angelina.'

'Well, your second name is Jane, and we shall call you that,' said the toys. 'You don't deserve such a pretty name as Angelina. We shall just call you plain Jane.'

Angelina was very angry. She went away and sulked. She thought the toys were the horridest she had ever known. Oh, if only she could live in a nursery, where everyone knew she was grand and beautiful, where she was called *Queen* Angelina and not plain Jane.

The toys were really a very kindly lot. The train was always willing to give Angelina a ride if she asked nicely, and the clockwork motor-bus would take her anywhere that she wanted to go. Even the goldfish in the big glass tank were kindhearted too, and once when it was very hot they let Angelina put on a bathing-dress and bathe in their water.

The toy sweet-shop man was always willing to give Angelina a sweet if she was hungry, and the panda often cooked her a nice little dinner on the toy stove. So you see Angelina had no right to grumble, for the toys were really very good to her. But they would *not* make her queen because she wasn't nice enough. And I really don't blame them–do you?

One day Angelina was so annoyed at being called Jane so often that she walked right out of the nursery and ran away. 'I shall go to another nursery where people will be nice to me!' she raged. 'I shall be queen somewhere else, even if *you* won't make me yours.'

She walked on for some way and at last came to a small house. She knew which the nursery was because of the bars across the window to stop the children from falling out. So up to the nursery she went and there she found a great many other toys, all most surprised to see her.

They thought she really was very beautiful – and so she was! Her hair shone in the sunlight and her eyes were as blue as forget-me-nots. When she smiled sweetly she was very lovely – but she didn't smile often enough!

'Good afternoon, toys,' she said. 'I've come to live with you – and if you like, I'll be your queen. You may count it as a great honour to have a queen as beautiful as I am.'

'Well,' said a big teddy-bear, politely. 'It's really very kind of you, madam – but, you see, we happen to have a queen already.'

'Where is she?' said Angelina, looking angrily round, wondering if there was another doll more beautiful than she was.

'There she is!' said the bear, and he pointed to a little straight-haired doll, with a sweet face, sitting in a chair. She was dressed in a blue cotton frock and was not at all grand, though she was really very sweet to look at.

'Pooh!' said Angelina rudely, walking over to the doll and staring at her. 'You don't mean to say *she's* your queen! Why! she's the plainest, commonest little thing I've seen for a long time!'

'I may be plain and common,' said the little doll, 'but I am queen all the same!'

Angelina was so angry that she quite forgot herself – and whatever do you think she did? Why, she smacked the other doll across the face!

At once all the toys rushed up, shouting angrily – but the little queen-doll waved them back.

'I'm not really hurt,' she said. 'Let this doll alone, please. I shall not punish her, but I will make a bargain with her. If she likes she can stay in this nursery and try to be queen. If you like her better than you do me, you can crown her and make her your queen.'

'Very well,' said the toys – but you should have seen how they glared at Angelina!

'I shall soon be queen, then,' said Angelina proudly. So she settled down in the nursery and looked round to see what toys were there.

Presently up came a small bear. 'Will you tie my bow on for me, please?' he asked. 'It's come off.'

'Certainly not!' said Angelina at once. 'I'm not here to tie bows on baby bears!'

The bear went off, and Angelina saw the little queen-doll put down her knitting and tie the bow for him very

neatly.

'What are you knitting?' asked Angelina, looking at the lovely red wool the little doll was holding.

'It's a scarf for the panda,' said the doll. 'He always has colds in the winter, you know, so I thought I'd knit him a scarf to keep his throat warm.'

'Good gracious, fancy spending your time knitting for a dirty panda!' said Angelina, in disgust.

'He isn't dirty,' said the doll indignantly. 'Black and white is his proper colour. He washes as often as you do!'

'Well, knitting doesn't seem to be a proper thing for a queen to do,' said Angelina.

'There is no reason why a queen should not be as kind or as helpful as anyone else,' said the little doll quietly. 'In fact, *I* think a queen should work even harder for other people than anyone else. She must set them a good example, you see.'

'Pooh!' said Angelina rudely. She couldn't think of anything else to say.

As soon as the toys found out that Angelina didn't mean to be kind or helpful in any way they soon treated her as she deserved. They wouldn't do *anything* for her at all! The engine tipped her out when she tried to go for a ride. The clockwork bus wouldn't turn even a wheel when she asked it to take her to the other side of the nursery.

'Can't you walk?' it said rudely. 'Haven't you got legs?'

The little man in the toy sweet-shop ran and smacked Angelina when she tried to take a sweet, and nobody, not even the little clockwork mouse, would cook her anything on the stove in the doll's house. Most of the toys refused to speak to her and nobody wanted to play or be nice. Yet they were perfectly sweet to the little queen-doll! The train took her everywhere, and the bus was always telling her she could have a ride. The sweet-shop man saved her his best chocolates; and dear me, you should have smelt the meals that the clockwork clown cooked on the stove! Most delicious!

Angelina soon saw that there was no chance of her being queen in that nursery. So she sulked and pouted all day. But no one took any notice of her. At last the little queen-doll went up and spoke gently to Angelina.

'Angelina dear, why don't you go home? I am sure you are unhappy here.'

'Yes, I am,' said Angelina, beginning to cry. 'You are all horrid!'

'No we're not,' said the little doll.

'And goodness knows why the toys have chosen a plain little thing like you for their queen!' sobbed Angelina. Then the panda came up and spoke.

'*I'll* tell you why she's our queen and we love her!' he said. 'It's because she's quite different from you! She doesn't think of herself all the time – she thinks of others. She doesn't mind whether she is beautiful or not so long as she is kind. She isn't vain like you – or selfish like you – or stupid like you. Yes, *stupid,* I say, for anyone that was in the least clever would soon see that *you* were not fit to be a queen! Just go away from here, please, and don't come back again.'

Poor Angelina! Sobbing bitterly she left the nursery and walked back to her own home. She was so ashamed of herself that she didn't know what to do. She crept into her own nursery, hoping that the toys would not see her. But they did!

When they saw her crying they came

running over in alarm, for they were very kind-hearted. 'What's the matter, Jane?' they cried. 'Are you hurt?'

'No,' sobbed Angelina, quite glad to hear herself being called Jane again. 'I'm not hurt – but I'm terribly ashamed of m-m-m-m-m-myself! I'm not fit to be a queen, I know that now. But do have me back again with you, just as plain Jane, and let me try to be nicer. I won't be horrid any m-m-more!'

'Of *course* you can come back,' said the kindly toys. 'We've missed you, even though you weren't very nice. We'll help you to be friendly if you really want to be. Cheer up and don't cry any more!'

Angelina wiped her eyes and tried to smile. It was lovely to be back with the toys in her own nursery again. She would, she really *would* be nice, and then perhaps they would forget how proud she had been and how she had begged to be queen.

So now she helps them and does all kinds of things for them. She is even knitting a coat for the baby doll! And I shouldn't be surprised one day if the toys begin to whisper among themselves and say that, after all, Angelina Jane would make a very good queen! Would you?

15

The Big Box of Chocolates

Peter Penny had been very good to old Dame Twinkle when she had hurt her foot and couldn't go out to do her shopping. He had run her errands every morning for a week, and she was very grateful.

'I want to give you a present, Peter Penny,' she said. 'I wonder what you'd like. You have been very good to me.'

'I don't want anything, thank you,' said Peter Penny, who had been very well brought up and knew that it was wrong to expect presents for kindness.

'Well, I'm going to give you something,' said Dame Twinkle, who had also been well brought up and knew that she must certainly show Peter Penny how pleased she was with his kindness to her. 'How would you like that big box of chocolate animals that is in Mrs. Peppermint's sweetshop?'

'Ooh!' said Peter Penny, his eyes opening wide. The big box of chocolate animals was perfectly lovely. All the little folk of the village had gone to look at it and had longed to have it. If Peter Penny had it he could give a party and his friends could all share the animals. It would be really lovely.

Dame Twinkle saw Peter's eyes shining brightly, so she at once went to Mrs. Peppermint's shop and bought the box of chocolate animals. Then she gave it to Peter Penny with her love.

He had a large net-bag with him, because he had to do his shopping that morning, so he thanked Dame Twinkle very much indeed, and put the box into his bag. Then off he went to do his

shopping. He bought bacon and saus-
ages, a pound of rice, a tin of cocoa,
some flowers and a new saucepan.
Everything was squashed into his big
net-bag and soon it felt very heavy.

Peter Penny went home through the Magic Wood. When he was half-way through, something dreadful happened. The bottom of his net-bag broke into a hole, and out fell the big box of chocolate animals on to the soft grass. Peter Penny was swinging the bag as he went and singing a very loud and merry song, so he didn't know what had happened. The saucepan in the bag stopped anything else from falling out. Peter Penny went gaily on, not knowing at all that he had lost his precious box of chocolates.

Now not very far behind him came Mrs. Twitter, who sold yellow canaries in her little shop. Always when she came through the Magic Wood she wished a wish, because sometimes wishes came true there. And today she wished her wish.

'I do wish I could find a nice present lying on the ground all waiting for me!' she wished.

And dear me, the very next moment what should she see on the ground but the big box of chocolate animals that Peter Penny had dropped! She gave a squeal of surprise and rushed at it in delight.

But when she saw what it was her eyes filled with tears. 'Chocolate!' she said. 'Oh dear, what a pity! Chocolate always makes me feel so sick. Whoever would have thought I'd find a box of chocolates when my wish came true!'

She picked up the box and carried it off. As she went she wondered what to do with it.

'I know,' she thought. 'I'll give it to old Mister Ho-ho. He's been ill in bed for a long time now, and I'm sure he would love to have a nice box of chocolate animals.'

So she went to Mister Ho-ho's, and left the box with the little maid, who at once took it to Mister Ho-ho.

He opened the box, and dear me, how his face fell when he saw what was inside.

'Chocolates!' he groaned. 'Would you believe it? Just what the doctor said I wasn't to have! What very bad luck! Oh bother, bother, bother!'

He lay and looked at them. Then he thought that it would be a very good idea to send the box to little Silvertip, the elf across the way. It was her birthday and he would like to send her something. He knew she was very fond of chocolates.

So he sent his little maid with the big box across the way, and she knocked at the door. 'A present from Mister Ho-ho,' she said when Silvertip opened the door.

The little elf screamed with delight and ran indoors with it. But dear me, when she saw what it was, she sighed and sighed.

'Look!' she said to her elfin husband. 'Another box of chocolates! That makes the fifteenth I've had today for my birthday. Whatever shall I do?'

'Well, if you don't want it, don't waste it,' said her husband. 'Let me take it to Mother Hooky for her little boy. He'll love all these chocolate animals.'

'But he's such a very, very *naughty* little boy,' said Silvertip, who didn't like the small boy at all.

'Never mind,' said her husband. 'Naughty or good, he'll like chocolates.'

172

So off he went and gave the box to Mother Hooky for Hoppy, her small brownie son.

She was pleased - but what a pity, when Hoppy came home from school he was so rude and naughty that she really could *not* give him the chocolates. She sent him straight to bed instead.

She sat and looked at the box. 'What shall I do with them?' she wondered. 'I can't eat chocolates myself, and if I leave them in the cupboard that naughty little boy will steal them. I know! I'll give them to that nice little Peter Penny. He has been so good to old Dame Twinkle lately, running all her errands for her, and I know he likes chocolates.'

So she went to Peter Penny's house. Nobody was in. There was no light anywhere. So Mother Hooky opened the kitchen window and popped the box on the table just inside. She smiled to herself and thought: 'I won't tell Peter Penny what I've done. He can just find them and wonder where they've come from!'

Now when Peter Penny had got home that morning, he had emptied his net-bag on the table and looked for the box of chocolates at once. He thought he would like to eat one of the chocolate bears. They did look so very nice.

But to his great disappointment and horror there was no box there! It was gone. Then he saw the big hole in the bottom of the bag and he guessed what had happened. How upset he was!

'What bad luck!' he said to himself. 'To lose that wonderful box of chocolates – the best one I've ever had in all my life! Oh dear, I suppose I must go all the way back through the wood to see where I've dropped it.'

Poor Peter Penny! He had his dinner and then off he went to see if he could find his lovely box of chocolates. He looked here and he looked there, he hunted in the wood, he hunted in the fields. But no matter how hard he looked there was no box of chocolates to be seen. It was quite gone.

Peter Penny was tired and miserable.

He couldn't help a few tears squeezing out on to his cheeks as he went home. He was very nearly home when he met Smarty the Gnome, who thought himself very clever indeed.

'What's the matter, Peter Penny?' asked Smarty, staring at Peter's tears in surprise.

'Oh, nothing,' said Peter.

'Tell me what's the matter,' said Smarty, who was always curious to know everybody's business. 'Has someone been teasing you?'

'Of course not!' said Peter, crossly. 'Do you suppose I'd be so feeble as to cry if somebody teased me?'

'Well, what's the matter, then?' asked Smarty, simply longing to know.

So Peter Penny told him all about how he had been kind to Dame Twinkle, and how she had given him the wonderful box of chocolates, and how he had lost them.

'It's the first reward I've ever had for being kind,' said Peter, sadly, 'and now I've lost it.'

'Oh, that's the way of the world,' said Smarty, at once. 'It doesn't pay to be kind, you know, because you hardly ever get anything back for it, and if you do, you're bound to lose it. No, my boy, you listen to my advice. Don't go bothering to do kind deeds. Just get what you can out of other people, and look after yourself! It doesn't *pay* to be kind and good.'

'It certainly doesn't seem to,' said Peter Penny. 'It's very hard to lose that lovely box of chocolates. I shan't bother to be kind to anyone again.'

He said good-bye to Smarty and went on. He hadn't gone very far when he saw old Mister Candleshoe, almost bent double under a big load of wood. Now Peter was really a very kind little fellow and his first thought was to go and help Mister Candleshoe.

Then he stopped himself. 'No,' he thought, 'I won't. Why should I help him? I shan't get anything out of it. As Smarty says, kindness doesn't pay.'

So he went right past Mister Candleshoe, and didn't even say 'good afternoon.'

But no sooner had he passed him than Peter Penny felt bitterly ashamed of himself and he went as red as a sunset sky. 'How horrid of me!' he thought. 'Am I so mean that I can't give a hand to an old chap like Candleshoe? What do I care if kindness is rewarded or not? I shall be kind because I want to be!'

So back he went and took Candleshoe's big bundle away from him. He carried it all the way home for him and then turned to go to his own cottage.

'You're a kindly fellow!' called Candleshoe after him. 'A rare, kindly fellow, you are, Peter Penny. May you get what you most want today!'

Peter Penny smiled a crooked little smile. 'What I most want is that perfectly lovely box of chocolate animals,' he thought. 'But that's gone for good.'

Then he stopped in the greatest

astonishment, for there, set on the kitchen table, was the very box of chocolates he had lost that morning. There it was, with no note, no message. How did it get there? Where did it come from? What a very extraordinary thing!

'Ooh!' said Peter Penny, in delight, picking it up. 'Ooh! Who says kindness isn't rewarded!'

He danced round and round the room in joy, and a chocolate bear fell out of the box. Peter Penny picked it up and ate it. It was delicious.

'Now to write out the invitations to my chocolate party!' cried the little fellow, happily. 'What fun we shall have!'

And when all his friends came to the party Peter Penny told them about the very mysterious way in which the box of chocolate animals had appeared in his kitchen, and they were really most astonished.

'You deserve all the good luck you get,' said his friends, hugging him. I think he does too, don't you?

16

Oh, You Crosspatch!

Theo and Kitty were playing together in the nursery. It was raining fast outside, and they were both feeling very cross. Nurse wouldn't let them go out, and they wanted to. So they looked sulky and were ready to quarrel at any minute.

'Let's play with my new engine,' said Theo to Kitty. 'We will wind it up and let it run round and round on my set of lines.'

'No,' said Kitty. I'm tired of your silly old engine.'

'It isn't a silly engine!' cried Theo angrily. 'It's a lovely one.'

'We'll play with my new doll,' said Kitty. 'Let's put on her lovely blue bonnet and pretend to take her out calling.'

'Pooh, what a silly game!'cried Theo. 'That's just like a girl to want to play a stupid game like that!'

'Oh, you crosspatch!' shouted Kitty, pointing at Theo.

'Crosspatch yourself!' said Theo, sulkily. 'I tell you I shan't play with your silly doll. You play with my engine, and be a big girl, not a stupid baby.'

Kitty turned her back on Theo, and took up her doll. She found the new blue bonnet, and saw that one of the strings was loose. So she went to Nurse's work basket and found a needle and cotton to sew it on with. But when she went back to her doll, the bonnet wasn't there!

'You've taken it, you horrid boy!'cried

Kitty, in a rage. 'Give it to me at once.'

'I shan't,' said Theo. 'You wouldn't play with my train, and I shan't let you play with your doll, so there!'

'You're a nasty, mean thing!' said Kitty, beginning to cry.

'Ooh, you crosspatch!' cried Theo. Then, oh dear me, what naughty children! What do you think they did? Why, Kitty suddenly ran over to Theo's railway lines and stamped on them, and Theo took the doll's bonnet from his pocket and tore it in half!

Then Kitty howled, and Theo stamped with rage, and Nurse came running in, in a great hurry.

'Oh, you naughty crosspatches!' she cried. 'You ought to be ashamed of yourselves! What have you done to poor Theo's lovely railway line, Kitty? See, you've bent them so much that he can't use them again. And he was so proud of them.'

'Theo tore my doll's new bonnet in half,' sobbed Kitty. Nurse looked at Theo and he hung his head.

'Oh, Theo, how could you do such an unkind thing? You knew how pleased Kitty was with that bonnet; well, really I am ashamed of you both. You can just go into different corners of the room, and stay there till you both feel better.'

Theo went into one corner and Kitty went into the other. Nurse cleared up their toys, and then went out of the room. The two children stood in the corners with their backs to one another – but they were both very unhappy.

'Poor Kitty!' thought Theo. 'I ought to have played dolls with her first, then perhaps she would have played with my engine afterwards. I'm sorry I tore that

bonnet – I know she liked it very much – and now it is quite spoilt!'

Kitty was thinking about Theo too. She loved him very much, and when she remembered how she had stamped on his railway lines and broken them, she grew red with shame.

'How could I have been so unkind to him?' she thought. 'Now he can't make his new engine run on lines at all, and he was so pleased when it did.'

So both the children stood there feeling sorry, but not liking to say so. And both of them suddenly decided to show that they really did love one another and hadn't meant to be so horrid.

Oh, You Crosspatch!

'I shall ask Cousin Dora if she would like to buy my new dolly, and if she would, I'll buy some new railway lines with the money,' thought Kitty. 'Then Theo will be happy again.'

'I shall ask the boy next door if he will buy my engine for fifteen pence, and if he would, I'll buy a new blue bonnet with the money,' thought Theo. 'Then Kitty will be happy again.'

So when Nurse came in and said the sun was shining, and they had both better go out and let the wind blow away their bad temper, the two children put on their hats and coats without a word. Kitty took her doll, and Theo took his engine.

Kitty ran down the street till she came to where her Cousin Dora lived. She told Dora what she wanted to do, and Dora, who thought Kitty's doll was the nicest in all the world, gave her twenty pence for it.

Kitty ran straight to the toy shop and bought a new set of railway lines. Then she hurried home again.

Theo went to the boy next door and sold his new engine for fifteen pence. Then off he went to the draper's and bought a lovely new blue bonnet for Kitty's doll. He hurried home again to give it to Kitty, and they met in the back garden.

'Kitty, I'm sorry I was such a crosspatch,' said Theo. 'Here's a new bonnet for your doll.'

'Oh, Theo! And I'm so sorry too,' said Kitty. 'Here's a new set of railway lines for your engine.'

'How did you get them?' asked Theo, in surprise.

'I sold my new doll,' said Kitty. 'How did you get the bonnet?'

'I sold my new engine!' said Theo – then the two children suddenly began to laugh.

'Oh, Theo!' said Kitty, at last, 'I can't put your bonnet on my doll, because I've sold her!'

'And I can't put my engine on your railway lines because I've sold it too!' said Theo. 'We've got a bonnet without a

doll and lines without an engine. Oh, what sillies we have been! Let's tell Nurse.'

So they ran off to tell Nurse. She listened and shook her head.

'Well, my dears, that's what comes of being cross and unkind,' she said. 'But I'm very glad you were ashamed of yourselves, and tried to put things right. It was nice of you both to buy something in place of the things you spoilt. Now, don't quarrel again.'

Nurse must have told Mother – because when Saturday came, two parcels arrived for the children. And what do you think was inside them? A lovely new doll to fit the bonnet, and a beautiful new engine for the railway lines. Inside was a card, and on it Mother had written: 'For my two little crosspatches!'

'We'll never be crosspatches again!' said Kitty, running to thank Mother.

'We never, never will!' cried Theo. 'Come on, Kitty – let's try the engine on the lines, and the bonnet on the doll!'

Back to the nursery they went, and as far as I know they have never been cross again!